AT THE END

of

THE WORLD

&

DREW'S WAR

AT THE END of THE WORLD

A Fractal Meta-Loco Narrative

in E-flat Major

&

DREW'S WAR

A Vietnam War Tale

Da Nang, 1967

by

Ted Cleary

Library of Congress Cataloging-in-Publication Data

Cleary, Ted. (E.F.) 1965—
    At the End of the World; Drew's War—1ˢᵗ Ed.

    ISBN 979-8-218-25506-0

        1. Ted Cleary—Fiction. 2. Apocalypse—Fiction.
        3. Jazz—Fiction. 5. Marcus Aurelius—Philosophy.
        6. Mob violence—Psychology. 7. Surfing—Fiction.
        8. Vietnam War—Fiction. 9. Black humor—Fiction.

Published by Silver Song Press, USA
Cover design: Mara Satori
Cover Image: *The Flying Dog of Lago de Atitlán*

Text version v12.2; Cover photo and artworks © the Author

Re the cover, that is a real-life dog bounding high off a wooden dock after a ball; taken from the pier of Casa del Mundo, across from volcanoes at Lago de Atitlán, Guatemala. No effects beyond color; serendipitous composition after about a dozen ecstatic canine launchings into the lake. The dog would have kept going all night.

Back cover: *Raining Bartletts on Mars,* pastel & charcoal on paper
Drawing p. 137: *Swan-Snake de Borges,* pencil on paper
Designed in the USA; printed wherever volume is offered for sale

Set in Dragamond: see Note on Type

TABLE OF CONTENTS

AT THE END of THE WORLD

A Fractal Meta-Loco Narrative

in E-flat Major

for Dave,

dweller of high places,
aeries,
 finisterres

— & who's ridden out plenty
of storms

Thou shalt be visited of the Lord of hosts with thunder, and with earthquake, and great noise, with storm and tempest, and the flame of devouring fire...the multitude of thy strangers shall be like small dust...

ISAIAH 29: 6—7

Do not act as if you were going to live ten thousand years. Death hangs over you. While you live, while you have the power, be good and righteous.

MARCUS AURELIUS

It's just as well we don't live forever—we'd waste even more time.

LUDWIG VON GEGENSCHEIN

1

Dean, the saxophone player, was dressed to kill—or to die, actually, considering the end of the world was at hand. His 174 pounds sported a snappy tuxedo, a freshly shaved face, and hair pulled back into a neat ponytail. Even though he knew he would not live past five o'clock on this December day, he was a happy man. He was a brink player, a master of improvisation, and today he would be playing the ultimate brink gig: Armageddon.

He removed the reed from his mouth and sniffed speculatively.

"Rubber again," he said.

The city had been burning for weeks. When the reports had first come, those sad government reports confirming the ravings of the prophets, the city had lost its mind. In fact, the whole planet had lost its mind, but Dean and the other revelers on the hill could not vouch for the planet. They could, however, vouch for the city.

It had begun with looting and then quickly escalated to riot, rape, and murder. Roving mobs, like rats sprung from electric cages where they'd been shocked and bewildered from birth, now funneled all that bloodshot rage into biting and rending something, anything, even themselves. They burned down their own neighborhoods first, leaving themselves naked and prey long before the mansions on the hills had even their first blackout or lost water for their sprinkler systems.

But in the last week, the shrines of wealth had been desecrated, savaged by an engine of hatred as old as money itself. Servants had fled, pointlessly stealing silverware—or had turned on their masters. Police largely evaporated.

The children of privilege, flaxen beauties with slim legs and unblemished skin, were dragged out by torchlight, violated, murdered, and fed to their cats. The richest of the rich—the lords of humankind with their severe countenances and icy calculating eyes—were butchered like pigs and hung ankles-up and dripping, spinning slowly like Mussolini hams from under the arches of their own impressive porticos.

2

None of these events, though, were of too much moment to the party on the hill. As the last mansion on the last street on the tallest bluff approachable by only the most sinuous of roads, it would be the final one to fall and might even make it to the Apocalypse itself without suffering the gross impertinence of murder at the hands of the underclass.

Secure behind twelve-foot walls and wrought-iron gates, the party at 1461 Finisterre Overlook had been going on for weeks—for as long as the riots themselves. Most guards had disappeared, but a few joined the party, and there were still plenty of guns.

There were dancers: flamenco and Turkish; musicians: jazz, calypso, even a string quintet. And despite so many days of indulgence and gluttony, there were still dizzying racks of fine wines in the cellar, wheels of rich cheese in the pantry, and—with the recent arrival of Lorenzo, the baker's son—an entire truck full of Italian breads and pastries.

"We should count ourselves lucky," said Mrs. Sexton, mistress of the hill, enthroned among wine-drinking guests in her vast, cathedral-like library; she sat with the regal assurance of a leopardess. "Our view is our security—and I don't just mean this eagle's nest on the mountain."

High above the open doors and facing each other down the long, ribbed nave of 87,000 volumes rose two huge moon-windows of clear, chiseled crystal—stained glass without the stains—but aglow with the hummingbird shiver of a prism.

"Perspective," she said, gesturing in a smooth orbit at the surrounding senate of books. "That's the sum total of everything recorded here."

Some sirens and muffled explosions reached them from way down the valley, mixed with the distant barking of dogs. Nearly everyone looked towards the open western door, which inhaled vague tendrils of smoke.

"So how are we lucky again?" asked a dazed woman with smudged mascara, slightly slurring her words. "How is anyone lucky?"

Mrs. Sexton ran a finger down her champagne flute and held the woman's gaze with her clear green eyes. Her silver hair was drawn back from her forehead; she spoke in sparkling paragraphs.

"In a world of no options, we are creating the context of our own deaths. Think of how few people in history have had that luxury. Even at war—where death is constantly at hand—there is no warning as to when it will strike. It may strike when the soldier is at prayer, stepping from a tent, or squatting in the fly-buzzing latrine. But we here are different. We know the place—and if the mob doesn't reach here first—we know the hour and the minute.

"And from that knowledge comes a choice: we can die with dignity, or we can die with fear."

3

Everyone knew what fear was—they felt it like a cold hand across their hearts—

but just what dignity entailed was open to interpretation. Some, like Mrs. Sexton, found it in remaining stately and poised, aristocratic, even if to do so was meaningless. *Omnium absurdum est.* Others prayed, trying to revive contact with a God who had long been forgotten in the crush of worldly distractions. Some wept in anguish, grieving wasted lives, talents, loves; some wandered Mrs. Sexton's prodigious library, dumbly fingering the spines of tomes unread and too short of time to read now; some reckoned their blessings, finding more to cherish than regret; some made themselves senseless with alcohol; others fucked themselves into oblivion.

O n this last count, Lorenzo, the baker's son, was in great demand. Nineteen years old and hopping with hormones, he'd been snatched from his truck like a carnival hobbyhorse by those women who wanted to go out with a bang and found himself riding and ridden from dawn to dusk and then straight through the night: the perpetual quest for the great orgasmic thunderclap.

A vigorous youth from forehead mane to taut springing flexors, he readily obliged these many keen, slightly-long-on-the-vine femmes with fierce tendons carved into their gorgeous cordovan necks.

He had often cruised the city's exclusive neighborhoods in his bread van, casting tantalized glances up long, curving drives to forbidding mansions. He'd heard the *thwa-pock* of tennis balls being hit somewhere behind the high ivy walls and imagined white shorts shifting over perfect, bouncing buttocks.

From merely spying from behind the wheel of his toaster-shaped truck, delivering focaccia and baguette-like *stilatos* for Il Forno de Centauro, he was now—his gold confirmation crucifix swinging up and rapping him between the eyes—driving inside such prime and pampered loins for up to ten hours a day—some seasoned, some tender, some wonder-worked into ageless ambiguity—but now all about to be thrust wholly beyond time into Eternity. Most copulated with breathless urgency, as if buried alive and clawing their way to the lung-sucking air.

They gobbled him like a bottle of Ecstasy.

Aware of doomsday, Lorenzo almost relished it, prepped for it as he'd been by a lifetime of dirt-bike jumps and bam-bam, gore-gushing video games; paintball and live-ammunition rifle ranges; tactical war play, and goth-metal thanato-riffs promising annihilation with every whip of the compact disc.

He could live, he could die, he didn't really give a damn. He'd never been more screamingly alive—and would hammer his way out through the other side.

4

A distance down the valley, on another hill, was the monastery of San Sebastián. Founded by a renegade sect of flagellating Carthusians at the turn of the last century, the monastery had survived by selling off chunks of the mountain to developers as the city crept ever upward into the highlands. The monastery was moved brick by brick in 1965 to its current site at the very top of the cliff, where it looked out over its smog-sickened mountain gardens to the sprawl of the city below.

The brothers on the hill were in rapture over the news of the Apocalypse. They felt a tonsure-tingling frisson to be on the earth for the Second Coming of Jesus Christ, an event that had been eagerly anticipated since 29 A.D.

So many generations had passed since Jesus made his MacArthurian promise that even the most ardent believers had been forced to promulgate specious theories explaining The Lord's curious conception of punctuality.

One monk, though, had never doubted the Lord. At least not since 1970 when the Lord ripped off half his face and left scars in the shape of a crucifix.

Brother Mark had been born on the severe flats of South Dakota where the wrath of God was in plain evidence. Lashed by the winds and scorched by the sun, he had grown up right-eous, following the path of Jehovah. He'd grown up straight and strong as a Black Hills hardwood but then had won a scholarship to an East Coast university and begun to stray.

It was 1967 and radicalism was sweeping the campus, and he did not have the wit to duck the rhetoric slung at him from all sides; con-sequently, his mind became a smudgy smear of slogans and sloppy thinking. His first denim-down, dorm room fellatrix undid him com-pletely, and he became, for a few short years, as sybaritic as a plainsman is capable of becoming. Flinging himself into the Carthaginian flesh-pots, he licked tabs of acid, he licked Aquarian oysters, he licked his past.

By some fluke, he found himself playing mandolin for a psychedelic blues band that made a trippy incoherent record and toured the country in a Day-Glo school bus. The bus was a cantankerous old beast and its axles groaned under the weight of instruments, amps, sandalwood swamis, and wide-eyed hippie love birds.

Never snugly in the in-crowd, Mark was patronized as something a rube by the trust-fund bohemians heading up the group, and after spending 1969 on the road, despite the pleasurable and near-permanent post-coital haze, the whole thing began to pall on him as slack and bombastic.

H e was contemplating quitting the band when God made his thinking easier by running the bus off a cliff in the Sierra Madres and plunging it ninety feet straight down into a stony canyon.

With the exception of Mark, every living thing on that bus—the band, the groupies, the insidious crotch crickets—perished in the ensuing fireball, thrusting them all into rock'n'roll history with a death so spectacular that it more than compensated for the blundering repertoire which might have otherwise consigned them to oblivion.

Decades later, the Gigantic Waxworks Indelible was still saluted over bongs on college campuses, revered as virtual avatars of acid rock. And Mark himself, the sole survivor of the holocaust, a lone Ishmael, was the subject of endless speculation, for shortly after being peeled from the rocks of the burning arroyo, he had disappeared completely, leaving behind him nothing but a few bloodstained bandages and a budding mythology.

5

In the belly of the valley, the tribes were mustering for assaults up the canyons and into the hills. The end was imminent, and the idolaters of Envy lusted to release the last of their spite before everything—their resentment, their unslaughtered victims, and they themselves—became nullified by the one-in-a-trillion trajectory of a blind and wayward comet.

Death was the great equalizer, true, but what they wanted to do—if even just for a minute, or for a bristling, hog-roaring second—was to hammer in the hurt, and to *be* for that one climactic moment, *at last* more equal than others. Among the rioting tribes, the pronouncements of the chieftains took on an inspired urgency, every word swollen with biblical grandeur. In these last days, the leaders were those best able to summon the language of the Apocalypse, inspiring the mob's faith that their anguished flailing was illuminated by some sort of radiant majesty—rather than merely shot blind with panic, like ants swarming beneath a stone.

A mos Flint, spearheading a skinhead contingent, was such a captain. Like Brother Mark, Amos had been raised by granite-hard Gideons, but unlike the monk, he was unhaunted by any ragged figure moving from tree to tree in the back of his mind—he had shot it dead like a pheasant. And too many years in Hollywood trying to hustle his skin and masks had gutted him of all conscience.

Standing atop a blackened Mercedes, amidst the smoking shells of cars and shattered televisions—a cleated Ahab a-hunt amidst pluming leviathans—Amos glared out at his shifting troop of stripling Nazis. He brandished a long Japanese sword—liberated from a fine collection, and as sharp as it had been in 1629. His eyes glittered with mischief.

27

"And behold, saith the Lord," he brayed. "I will kill her children with death—and send upon them the sword, the famine, the pestilence, the whirlwind. Behold yon rivers of blood, bitter like black honey—and the legions of locusts and greenbottle flies—teeming and swarming, devouring corpses and trees and heaven itself—"

L ike many, Amos had come west to manifest his destiny in the movies—or failing that, in television; or failing that, in advertising or soaps. Stardom—even minor stardom—had seemed possible, probable, *and even*—when he'd just sucked in a deep draught of uber-cranked 29% THC wacky weed—downright *inevitable:* he had some theatrical chops, was fit and *cut*—and his headshots were crisp and well-lit. *He was good to go.*

But many are called and few are chosen.

O California! ye slush pit of wasted talent—all that ripe and overripe fruit softening and bubbling and bursting into sick syrup under the sun. He'd gone to a vast blur of readings and auditions and screen tests; he'd played bit parts and puked out lines of stunning vapidity—his biggest hit had been an ad for a 5-bladed pivoting razor—but for any film longer than a student short, the peppermint-gum casting directors and oiled-ringlet producers barely suppressed yawns as they waved their hands for him to stop—*OK that will do—Next!*

You're not quite what we're looking for—the repeated wasp sting to the inner ear—impersonal, vague, but also personal, rankling. *You* are not quite it. *You.* Are not quite It. *You.*

But in the sudden gatecrash of these End of Days, he'd landed his leading role—captain of this band of savage orphans—and the media moguls had discovered that their empires of flesh and fantasy were mere soap bubbles and peacock plumes.

Just days before, Amos had savored the exquisite delectation of lining up a half-dozen pleading and yabbering industry heads and decapitating them all—and had even filmed the sequence for an off-the-cuff *cinéma vérité* piece—*Helter Skelter, The Final Chapter*—which would alas remain unfinished due to formidable technical difficulties including the comet strike.

And yet further glorious bloodletting awaited Amos in the highlands: he was done being an extra: this was his star turn, his shining moment. He was showing the world what guts and chops he had—cue thunderous applause.

A mos continued his strut on the crumpling Mercedes roof: "So tell me, why do the heathen rage? Woe to them who recognize me not! And he that blasphemes and keepeth company with harlots—hear this: I brake the jaws of the wicked and pluck the spoils from his crooked teeth. Ribs I crack with iron, skulls I crush with stone!"

His troop was looking up in dumb wonder, cued by his gestures and guttural growls, moved by his grunts and spits and riffs and runs—but barely comprehending the meaning: he could have been speaking German. Like other fire-brands in this Spenglerian twilight, he was speaking in the forked and flippant tongue of expedient hate.

All that mattered was emotion, image, and impulse. These moved the crowd—knowledge he had little, scruples he had none. He could urge murder or mercy with equal passion and change positions on a whim. In the space of a day, or an hour—or upon the slightest hinge of a semicolon—he could incite a riot or quell it; defend a nation or slay it; spare a child or have it slit from crotch to collarbone. He was firmly of the School That Did Not Give a Shit.

As he looked out on the mob, the phalanx-führer smiled: he knew that he could just as easily have been the evangelical shepherd of a pious and righteous flock as the *kommandant* of these hollow-eyed misfits with swastikas cut into their foreheads.

The little lost pieces of trash. They would be scarred for life, yes, but given that the sky was split open and the clappers of doom in swing, their disfigurement would be brief, meaningless, too short-lived to have any consequences.

He laughed and saluted into the inferno.

Ah, ye skinheads with no skin in the game.

6

I t had been the very horror and immutability of permanence that had prompted Mark to flee the Sierras and vanish from sight. Upon smashing through the windshield, Mark had had most of his face sheared off and it didn't take a surgeon to tell him that he was finished with being a minor rock star. He stared at the mirror, his lidless eyes recoiling from the swift and terrible work of Jehovah. He was a curse, an astonishment, a hissing—an abomination in the sight of God.

Scourged by dread and shame, he fled the hospital, and sought purification in the desert. Out among the red rocks he was a wild man, feeding on scorpions and cactus flowers, sleeping in the shelter of a zeugen.

All blazing day, the sunburned sand melted into glass; moonless nights, Saturn stared, a cool panopticon. *The voice of the Lord breaketh the cedars and divideth the flames of fire.* A swollen rattlesnake seized its own tail—and then, in slow peristaltic gulps, ate itself whole; upon its final bite, its overstuffed head popped in a belch of benzene.

After forty days his delirium passed. He raised a heap of stones, and with his way pointed out by Joshua trees, he followed a long barefoot camino west to the city of angels, where he found the monastery and his anonymous place among the ascetics. They took him in without a word.

Though he still sometimes awoke to the terror of plunging through spinning space, his chaos solidified with routine. He cultivated the mountain garden by day and studied ancient manuscripts at night; he bathed each morning before sunrise. His weeks were marked by a ritual round of silence, renunciation, and penance.

D ecades passed. Mark aged but his face never healed. Indeed, his scars became more vivid, bright as blood. *Stat crux dum volvitur orbis.* When the news of the end came and the smoke rose to blacken the grapevines, Mark smiled, pleased to see confirmation of the doom he had always felt, and to see retribution visit the venal swarm of sinners below him. As he looked out over the wall, he touched his scars with trembling fingers. *He that hath ears, hear; that hath eyes, see.*

7

D own in the valley, in the heart of his gang's ancestral turf, Qelvin Lee, the warlord of the Skels, was rallying his posse for a final day of rage and revolution. Unlike Amos Flint, the neo-Nazi, Qelvin expressed no amusement in his lips and eyes. This blankness was not for a want of humor in the moment, but rather in the man. Although only twenty-four, he'd hardened into a V.I. Lenin mummified by clench-fisted hate, his innate warmth burnt out by polemics so fierce that no subtlety could survive its fire.

Qelvin's ascendancy to the helm of the city's most violent gang would have surprised those who had cooed him as a child. The only issue of prosperous lawyers, he'd been raised amidst plush pillows, pads, bolsters, and shams, yet was increasingly rankled by a root indignation that he'd come to ascribe—after much dogged evangelism by his freckled, red-haired tutor—to his race. That this dermal diagnosis seemed unwarranted given his most liberally *included* up-bringing made it even more unbearable. Deeply ashamed of his bath-oil-and-BMW background, he sabotaged it at every turn and was ejected from one leafy private school after another.

His devolution had begun at fourteen when he was at an orientation for The Center for Gifted and Affluent Youth. The amiable moon-faced director sat everyone in a circle and posed the safe and spongy question of What They Wanted To Be When They Grew Up.

After the cross-legged teens reeled off their earnest ambitions of activist, environmentalist, and documentary filmmaker, Kelvin punctured the moment with his blunt admission that he wanted to fuck a woman up against a wall. The director's face twitched, and after a strained remainder of the morning, Qelvin was gently relieved of further participation in the program.

Qelvin's career progressed to his satisfaction, and the crowning moment of his young life came when he was expelled from the last and worst school in the city—where he'd met some of his future boys—and after some shrewd reconnaissance of various hoods, took up residence with the drug-dealing Skels.

Because he clearly wasn't *Street*—something obvious at a sniff—he had to work triply hard to win respect, which he accomplished by being icicle cruel and diamond smart.

A few years later, he captured leadership by snapping a bullet into the eye of the reigning gang lord during a debate turned bad over turf expansion policy. The kingpin, Kool P., was pushing for openly grabbing enemy territory, but Qelvin quietly argued for caution. Losing face, the irate capo pulled a gun, but Qelvin swiftly iced the matter with an impressive 9mm hipshot through P.'s astonished iris.

Qelvin proved himself the wiser because the other gangbangers slaughtered each other over the summer, and the Skels, never losing a man, sat out the war and simply strolled out and seized the streets after the other gangs collapsed.

They became rich beyond their wildest dreams of avarice and were poised for even greater expansion—the L.A. basin, California, and beyond—when their incipient empire (like everything else) was suddenly to be snuffed out beneath the shadow of the comet.

8

W here God was throughout all the turmoil and despair of these last days was a matter of great conjecture. Some said He had caused it, some said He was just letting it happen, some quoted their entire stock of Nietzsche and said He was dead.

"God, I'm afraid," said Mrs. Sexton, "has nothing to do with it. And poor Friedrich, even less." She bit lightly into a slice of apple and listened to the Bach fugue being played in an alcove. She continued her thought.

"It's all a matter of orbits and gravity, nothing else. It happened before, it will happen again. Whom did the brontosaurus blame? And the great T-Rex? To drag the concept of God into it at this late hour is anachronistic, not to mention embarrassing."

I n the dusky cool of the wine cellar, out of hearing, was a pool of lamentation. The perpetually surprised were weeping about the cruel unfairness of life. The many bottles in their rows, honeycombed and catacombed, and extending far into the curving gloom, gazed on stoically and offered no comment.

9

A long with the monks of San Sebastián and a few dismal souls whose aesthetic included the bruise-purple beauties of suicide,

Dean, the saxophone player, was looking forward to the end of the world. This anticipation, however, derived from no morbid fascination: it arose from the impetus it would give his art.

He was a musician who performed most brilliantly in contexts where sanity and tonality seemed in the gravest danger of extinction. Several years earlier, he had been the leader of the Creedmoor Quartet, a group of five jazz players with histories of demonic possession. Although their number was five, they refused to acknowledge this in their name for fear of attracting the pentangular forces of Satan.

Dean relished sessions with these players, their techniques perfect but their ideas diabolical—several leagues beyond bizarre by even the most esoteric standards—the tonal center of their pieces forever spinning off into disparate and incongruous corners of the musical sound garden. While the madmen ran wild like panicked horses, bastards of tonality, Dean gave chase and circled them, darting, dodging, dropping notes at their feet, framing harmonic shims for their manic micro-tones and half steps.

To some degree perhaps, Dean's balancing role had been foreordained, had been tapped into the spinning rims of fate by his having been born a leap-year child, a baby slapped alive on the 29th day of the shortest month, on that little shimmy of sunlight wedged into the winter quadrennial—to keep true the Gregorian cycle, to keep the wheels of time from wobbling over-much on its pitted road through the human mind.

And on this day, the last day, he was looking to shore up more than music or calendars: he was looking to shore up the foundations of the whole collapsing world.

10

U pstairs, in one of the tastefully appoint-ed bedrooms, Lorenzo, the baker's son, was being used (willingly, true) for his sex. Having already shot the clematis six times that day, his huevos were howling and his rooster was as sore as a peeled finger.

Marisa felt him plowing into her as he'd been doing for the last hour, and though she wished he were more inspired, she didn't want him to stop. She was estrous and hungering for seed. She imagined the egg slipping into place, snug, receptive, welcoming the millions of thrashing sperm, the swimmers in the secret sea.

Marisa, in fact, was desperate to become pregnant. Ever since the news of the comet had thrown the world into disarray, Marisa had thrown her legs open to any man who would have her. And since sex is never very far from a man's mind—even on the very eve of dooms-day—she'd had many takers. She had wrapped herself around over a dozen men and quietly thought she might have conceived on the previous Friday. She had awakened feeling different—a kind of density in the uterus, an accretion of cells—the rapid and relentless drive of biology—barely appreciable, naturally, but perceptible nonetheless.

The feeling was familiar because Marisa had been pregnant before. Years earlier, when she was still a student, she'd been "spontaneous" with a guitar-playing bartender who did not withdraw in time. She did not know him well and when she went to his job to tell him, he said he was sorry but there was nothing he could do.

He gave her whatever was in the tip jar—a few dimes shy of thirty bucks—and wished her well. On her way home, she dropped it all into the cup of a homeless woman sitting in the rain singing "Monday, Monday" with a ruined voice.

The woman cast Marisa a ragged blessing, a ravaged *God bless you, God bless you,* and Marisa walked on. She walked blindly, her brain numbing, praying that the woman's blessing would also extend to whatever little creature it was growing in her womb that would be flushed out in the following days.

She wouldn't have thought that she would miss that little cluster of cells, that embryonic toehold that was with her for only a month, but she did. She felt sad and empty, deserted like a street after a parade. They rinsed her with saline and that was the end of it.

"Delenda Carthago est," she said.

Lorenzo paused in his hip thrusting.

"Say what?"

Marisa looked at Lorenzo, the boy flushed and sweating.

"Just come into me," she said. "Gush into me, give me babies."

That's all it took. He came furiously—pumping, spurting, awhirl with visions of fecundity.

11

The last time Mrs. Sexton had suffered the marriage bed was over twenty years earlier. She had always thought of sex as something of an imposition, and as she'd been born rich, and had also enjoyed—with even rarer luck—some success as a novelist, it had never been a strict poker-play necessity.

Not that she begrudged the younger generation their obsession with sex. She made no comment on the stress and strain the house was enduring under the weight of desperate, last-minute fornication. Naturally, it wasn't pleasure they were after—but distraction, deliverance. Tragic mammals, reason wrapped in flesh, let them enjoy themselves—for soon they would know.

"Of course," she said, musing on her own past, "those were different times."

She had spent her youth the object of lust and conquest by countless men, but she had spurned them all. She'd been to enough estate auctions to know that the truly priceless objects are never on offer; she would never put herself in the false position of a man's fumbling grasp.

So she had outgrown her youth untouchable—and virtually untouched; and when, in a moment of rose-fading doubt, she finally consented to marriage (to a well-placed but frankly fungible pink financier), her sex life was—it cannot be denied—anticlimactic. Her husband had an erratic, skittish member that either sprayed her thighs prematurely or failed to engorge at all.

After waiting a year for this man to post a sturdy sentinel—this man who bought and sold third world countries over lunch—she suggested he find another bedroom. She slept alone, she and her cat, and her husband moved down the hall.

She then commenced building her prodigious library and he bought an apartment in town where he could receive various mistresses and carnal-charmers who channeled all their powers to conjure life from his bedeviled loins.

Mrs. Sexton knew of his cookie pad and did not object. Indeed, she approved. Much better that harlots and starlets cooed over his capricious flighty organ: she could study architecture and read and write in peace. The extravagant lengths to which he bumbled after ecstasy diminished him, and with each spasm wheedled from his dizzy, overstimulated mushroom, her freedom steadily increased.

H er library unfolded magnificently, with inherent discipline and proportion, foliating into an elegant, light-filled, intimate cathedral of the mind—a personal chapel to the logos. When she read, she sat legs-up on a fine silk couch, but when she wrote, she stood fully alert, shoulders-back at a mahogany lectern with inlaid braids of gold; and when the ink flowed from her pen, effortless and seemingly unbidden, it was as if it flowed through her and from her, a river of crisply apprehensible signs and symbols.

On the library walls, the hands of clocks flew backwards or forwards—or, then forgotten, disappeared entirely—and in those seabright minutes she swam fluidly with the stitched-and-sewn sentences around her, folio voice and leaf-stream, in the quicksilver river of Eternity.

12

Down in the valley raged the riot of fear. The fires were burning anew, brighter in the mountain shadows and spread by both the wind and the hands of arsonists. Trees, grass, roofs, homes—they all went up in the blaze. The rich died tangled in their badminton nets, shot down as they fled their homes.

A t 841 San Pablo Way, Qelvin Lee, the leader of the Skels, sought to live out (yet again) his pubescent fantasy. In the past days, he had nailed more than one woman up against the wall—and this house, this fine mansion with its Andalusian walls—was making him adamantine with its promise of violence.

He heaved a concrete cistern through a ground floor window and climbed inside. Doors slammed on the floor above and he pursued. With pistol raised, he kicked in the door of the master bedroom and was stopped dead not by a bullet but by the shock of recognition. The couple hugging each other across the room were staring at him too.

"Kelvin Lee," said the woman, surprised? relieved? horrified?

Kelvin was suddenly hobbled by his history and an insidious politeness.

"Mrs. Lucas," he said. "Mr. Lucas."

"I know your mother," said the woman.

"We've known your mother for twenty years."

"She's a good woman," added the man, lamely. "Irene Lee."

Kelvin shot him a look. A look of *extreme* admonition. A look that labored to convey the complex urgency of the situation: here was Qelvin, fulfilling the role of *fearsome feral predator,* smeared with blood and adrenalized for murder, confronted by a couple who had known him as a boy—who had given him rides on their knees, had read to him out of oversized picture books, and had clapped with generous warmth as he'd blown out his birthday candles.

How could he shoot such people?

Voices from downstairs. Yo! Qelvin, yo!

Kelvin was hamstrung by his reserve of conscience and stood twitching in the doorway, begging for an excuse to kill them. One irritating word, one scintilla of condescension, one overwrought appeal to their past friendship—these or any number of poor choices would have triggered swift terminal ballistics for Mr. and Mrs. Lucas.

As the couple paled, staring at the muzzle and Kelvin's trembling index finger, Kelvin was feeling the crushing onus of being a gang leader. He could never extend mercy in thought or deed—especially not in front of his boys—lest they learn cowardice and discretion (both detestable things).

All of which made the immediate moment more terrible because both Kelvin and his prey could hear the Skels trashing the floor below and thundering up the stairs like maddened buffalo.

"Yo, Qelvin! Qelvin! You still here?"

Kelvin looked at the Lucases again, so forlorn in their thin cashmere sweaters, and tightened his grip on the pistol.

They didn't flinch.

"Good," said Kelvin quietly. "If you started crying, I might've capped you."

"YO, QELVIN!"

"I'm out of here," said Kelvin, and shot a couple holes in the ceiling.

He met his troops halfway down the hall.

"Let's go," he ordered. "I killed 'em all."

13

Sometime around noon or one, in the cold water shower room of the monastery, Brother Mark milked the macaque for the last time. He picked the stall with the drain in the trough so that the evidence would flow neither east nor west into the stalls of his neighbors.

It was a delicate thing, this morose and furtive monolactation. Everyone did it, especially in the monastery, but it was better if no one had to look upon another man's private shame floating by in sad monastic clumps.

He closed his eyes and tightened his grip; he imagined golden-hipped Babylon offering up her sweet and pearly crimson. *Without filth there can be no cleanliness*, he incanted, and let fly his spirit lode.

* * * *

L orenzo rolled off Marisa and promptly fell asleep, his brain awash with opiates. Marisa clenched herself shut, feeling the warmth of his sperm seep into her. Then, she too fell asleep, and her muscles relaxed. The seed flowed out like water.

14

H is reverie punctuated by shouting and the crackle of gunfire, Dean was playing, swaying, spinning notes from his horn and thinking of his father. His father had been a drunk, a cop, and had an emotional range spanning from irritability to frothing rage. He resented his wife's college degree and Dean's talent for music.

As a child, Dean played the piano non-stop—for about ten hours a day. By the time he was nineteen, Dean was a master, having tunneled through classical and jazz and come out in a strange new country of dissonance and musical arrhythmia—the antipodes of pop.

Unfortunately, his father, whose aural sensibility was restricted to wheezy jukebox ballads and the clinking of ice cubes in a whiskey glass, had no use for his son's forays into the unknown. He was in no way pleased to have spawned a musical Magellan; he would have been happier had Dean taken the police test and plopped like a dab of butter into the civil service groove like his entire lineage. But no, he had a *prodigy* on his hands, a skinny little punk who wouldn't even humor his old man by playing a straight version of Auld Lang Syne on New Year's Eve.

One night Dean's father came home tanked on Wild Turkey and Bud, pissed from having lost six hundred bucks on a football game. He felt another surge of spleen upon seeing his wife—a former cheerleader turned flesh dirigible—docked in the kitchen, digging into blueberry pie with purple lips.

"Look at you rooting like a pig for God's sake. Don't you think you eat enough?"

His wife hardly looked up. "Drop dead, you dumb lush."

The impulse of divorce flashed across his mind for perhaps the ten-thousandth time, but—like every time before—the rebellious thought was instantly squashed by the knowledge that he'd forfeit his apartment and half his salary, losses he could ill afford as he could barely cover his gambling debts as it was. Better to keep his wife than lose his kneecaps, he was thinking. And the courts, the hassles, the bullshit—the torture never ends. No easy outs for the working man.

And this little fairy kid and his piano—he could hear it from here, the trash noises, that *garbage* he called music. And after all the fancy lessons. Dean's father made better music slapping down the toilet lid and blowing Guinness-inflected dung out his bunghole.

"Why can't you play a goddam *song* like everyone else?"

Dean continued playing, not responding. This did not surprise Dean's father, as the boy had not spoken to him in three years. The music went on, maddening, stilted, dissonant.

"Stop that. Stop that *shit* you're doing."

Dean did not stop.

The policeman started towards Dean.

"This is *my* house and that's *my* piano that I bought with *my* money because *your mother*"—he wrung out the word as if it were a putrid piece of meat—"because *your mother* said it would be *good for you.*"

He grabbed at the keyboard lid, intending to slam shut the piano.

"Don't touch the piano."

Terse, cold, matter-of-fact.

The first words out of his mouth in three years.

"What?"

"Don't touch the piano," said Dean. "You are a drunken ape. Apes and monkeys don't touch pianos."

Another surge of paternal spleen; the father's vision swirled with a swarm of white dots. He grabbed the boy by the collar and heaved him to his feet.

57

"Who you calling a monkey! Who the *fuck* you calling a monkey!"

"You," said Dean, calmly. "I'm calling *you* a monkey. *And* an ape."

Dean's father pushed the boy roughly and turned his wrath on the piano.

"I'll show *you* who's a monkey! I'll show *you* who's a goddam ape!"

He reached into his belt and fired five quick shots at the piano—*pap! pap! pap! pap! pap!* Bullets pocked the wood, leaving wounds of gold. Dean removed his fingers from his ears and could hear the piano wires singing.

"Very good," said Dean. "That was almost musical."

Dean's father stood frozen where he was, white-faced, still pointing the gun.

15

*L*oss is nothing but change, and change is the delight of Nature. A few days after his father shot the piano, Dean traded his keyboards for a saxophone and headed west. He was twenty years old. Along the way, in the various towns and cities, he sniffed out the musicians and learned to play. In St. Louis, he hooked up with four graduates of an insane asylum and formed the Creedmoor Quartet. They alienated even the most advanced members of the *avant-garde* and found themselves locked out of every venue in Missouri, whether reputable or not.

The only thing for it was to go where they would not be known, and California seemed the most obvious place to reinvent. They hopped a westbound freight outside the stockyards and holed up in an empty boxcar, which was filled with nothing but scraps of hay, manure, and the ghosts of cattle.

O ne morning, after a couple days of hearing the wheels singing and clicking beneath him, Dean awakened with a straw tickling his ear. He'd been deep in a dream: a silver dog, joyous, was sailing high over a lake, over a volcano, trailing a long saxophone line into the sky.

He sat up, unusually refreshed. All about him lay his friends, still sleeping, the pale light of dawn seeping in to cloak them in a thin blue blanket. The smell of dried manure was a tonic to his nostrils and Dean smiled, brightly alive in the sway and rattle of the train. He suddenly realized that all their previous music had been shite. Ugly, arrhythmic, and haughtily obscure.

The old man.

"Total garbage pretension," said Dean, dismissing the past, and picked up his sax. And then, in a boxcar of sleeping musicians jaded from years in the tonal void, he began to play. Real music, the good shit.

The others aroused and rubbed their eyes in perplexed wonder, as startled as they'd have been had they awakened on a raft far out at the sea.

They reached for their instruments with the giddiness of those who have just recovered their hearing. In a couple minutes they were all playing, harmonizing and delirious, the rhythm of the rails pounding out time like the pulse of life itself. Another thousand miles and they rolled into Los Angeles, a fully arrived jazz band. Success touched them for close to five years and they basked in warmth and light and money. They could not make a mistake musically and cut two sterling records.

B ut then the earth skipped the needle in its track and the band began to stumble. The music hitched and luck abandoned them.

Within three years, heroin had claimed two of the musicians, a car-crash a third, irreversible insanity the fourth.

Only Dean was left, but barely. He became unmoored and was blown aimlessly over the face of the deep. He slept in a box and had musical ideas that his fingers could not realize. They were like the insane, turning circles in doorways, babbling and foolish.

Then the news of the comet came, bringing order to the disorder: the swift finality of the impact would put an end to the chaos. Sense came back to Dean. He picked up the sax and learned to play it for the third time. He was touching thirty. Phrasing returned like refugees after a long war, tentatively at first, but then in waves. His mind became loud with the clamor of recovered memory.

And now, in these days of twilight and destruction, Dean's playing had never been better—he was king of the wastelands groove. He'd been up for three days and it hardly showed. As the crackle of gunfire became louder and closer in the arroyo, Dean's fingers flew fanatically up the keys, taking himself, the song, and the band into places of stunning freshness and beauty. He would ride this baby till the end of the world.

16

Mrs. Sexton had untold millions in the bank, in gold and silver bullion, in prime Iowa farmland, and it didn't bother her a whit to lose it all. Or even her life.

"We've always been suspended over the void," she said. "Always. Forever. Cotton Mather's dangling spider, Bede's storm sparrow flashing through the fire-bright hall, flitting from darkness to darkness. Once we were not—and to Not we shall return. Somewhere we know that. We do. The only difference about today is that the scaffolding has been stripped away and we are tumbling into the pit."

Lorenzo, recharging his rocky mountain oysters, sat among several women in the library, cradling a Quintarelli and drowsily listening to Mrs. Sexton. He was shirtless olive and gleaming with oil, adorned with a wreath of hyssop flowers and bay laurel—five women had been playing the sack of Rome. He wanted to listen—it seemed Mrs. Sexton was saying something important—but his endorphinated bloodstream was so awash with dopamine, oxytocin, and wine that he could barely keep his eyes open.

A night or two before, with a flashlight, the silver-haired hostess had led him and a few others up to the roof, where from a small platform, they looked out over the ruined city. All across the valley and tapering down the

boulevards into a far vanishing point of neb-
ulous glare, blazes flickered and smoldered like
the campfires of an enemy army. Long plumes
of smoke blew sideways towards the hills.

But up here in the heights, in the blackout night,
the sky was clear, a medieval blue modulating to
black—and spread high across that dome,
shimmering and pulsing like sparks, from the
mirroring sea to the mountains, was the
diamond spray of infinite stars.

In the long river of time, some lights might
have already winked out—or exploded in
world-making profusion—but no one had ever
known. And now for sure no one would ever
know.

The stargazers stood there for a long time,
silently, letting whiskey and cognac roll over
their tongues. The tips of their cigarettes glowed
like fireflies. Down below they could hear the
bass and drums, and Dean's baritone, playing a
blues so deep, so slow, with so much space

between the beats, that the horn could unwind a long easy line of hooks and growls to reel in the whole sobbing mystery of the world.

Lorenzo was beginning to drift—the stars, the fireflies, the flares on the plain like animal eyes—his own eyes were melting back into his brain. Sense was becoming nonsense, and nonsense becoming sense. He heard a voice behind him—a Turkish girl: "Behold the creation and resurrection—it's easy for Allah," And someone else quite close: "Our birth is but a sleep and a forgetting," Someone laughed. *"No hay río fácil. Habrá sangre en las orejas."*

Lorenzo jerked awake; he was back in the library. He sat up blinking and straightened his wine—it had been just about to spill.

"And remember the words of my dear Marcus," Mrs. Sexton was saying, gently placing her own wine next to a warm nugget of native copper, raw and ragged like molten coral.

"He said it doesn't matter how long we live or how soon we die. We can die today, tomorrow, next month, or after a thousand years—it doesn't matter. Everyone loses the exact same thing: the present moment, that's it. That's all we ever lose."

Lorenzo leaned towards a bright-eyed Sabine who'd vigorously bitten purple horseshoes into his neck that morning. "Who's Marcus?"

"Marcus Aurelius," whispered the woman. "She's mad about him."

Lorenzo nodded, grunting. "Her lover or something?" The woman was beginning to smile when Mrs. Sexton continued.

"There's no past, there's no future," she said. "They don't exist. Never did, never will. And since they don't exist, we can't lose them. We can't lose what we never had. Three more days and we'd reach the new year, but so what? *The only thing we can ever lose is the present moment—*"

and here she snapped her fingers, "the present spark of consciousness."

"Amen to that," said Lorenzo, raising his glass.

17

Qelvin Lee, the curtain-falling captain of the Skels and ultimate scourge of all things living and dead, stood locked in a blood-flecked bathroom, a little short of breath, examining himself critically in the mirror, firming up the tiniest tremors of weakness with scimitar cruelty and dogma. He would have to—*have to*—remain ruthless to the end. No compromise. No quarter. None.

But what had happened back there?

He instantly suppressed an upsurge of images about his parents and childhood—he squashed them fiercely down the memory hole. He could not afford such consciousness.

But fountain-like, they spurted up elsewhere: warm eyes and faces, welcoming words. He shoved them down, down, but they splashed back up—jets of impudent and unwanted warmth.

Blinking, he momentarily forgot himself. *What if he'd been…? What if all this…?* Snapping off the thought, he battered the images into submission again—beat them down, stuffed them away.

His pulse had risen but he reined it back in. He could have no doubts now—he'd have to see his great project, his unrelenting ahistorical rage, all the way through to its painful and marrow-spattered end.

18

A t long last, Amos Flint was on tour, burning up stage after stage in a Shermanesque path of glory up the long canyon. His guerilla troupe had been baptized in blood, with many lost, but it now reached for even greater heights.

Amos revolved and slow-danced atop a charred police car, elegantly slicing the air with the sword as if in a shadow duel with samurai—the blade flashed like a bleached bone. All about him the mob was shifting and bucking like stallions, eager to get on with it: the race, the hunt, the hurt. But restraint feeds even greater pleasure—and then, finally, Amos stopped his dance.

"Hearken now," he shouted, "the Kingdom of Death is at hand! He shall come as a thief, He shall come a raging fire, He shall come a thundering horseman slashing the vengeful sword! He shall visit his wrath upon the heathen and the Hittites! He shall send them all howling headless to Hell, pinioned butchered broken-boned to the backs of heaving beasts!"

A cloud of smoke billowed past the car, cloaking him for a moment.

"Down with all swine or kine or rodentine not of the master race!"

He gazed around at his unruly flock and noticed that he had attracted more than just churlish white boys with shaved heads and tattoos. In the swelling surge he detected a diverse range of skin tones and faces amidst the livid pallor, and so shrewdly veered off into the rhetoric of inclusion.

He stood even taller, lifting his chin. "The *master* race," he bellowed magnanimously, "is the *human* race—and each one of us is in it!"

The mob roared its approval, drowning out any confused dissent from his chalky striplings.

"Down with the old order of greed and oppression! Down with cynical division and setting brother against brother, race against race! Though the prophesied doom is here, we must do God's work of equity and justice! This is the final chapter, the last page—indeed the last letter of the last word! The final stroke!

"We must smash the bastions of silver— and through the ribs of kings, hammer stakes of gold! We must pave the way for the thousand years of equality and the brotherhood of man!"

The crowd roared again, tasting the end of foreplay and the unleashing of hot spasmic violence.

Amos paused a long tantric second to soak it all in. It was so beautiful he almost couldn't stand it. He licked the smoke from his lips and blinked lazily like a cat in the sun: this stage of the world—with all its splintered fractal pain, its agonized writhing lust, and its wild contending grace—would soon blaze up in most glorious annihilation.

Amos pointed his sword.

"To the hills, brothers! To the hills!"

19

B rother Mark, standing on the parapet, saw the masses surge up the hill and smash themselves like the sea against the foot of the cliffs. In them he saw, across over a thousand years, the Vikings sacking the rocky outposts of Ireland, greasy and stinking, gorged on meat and the plunder of Irish hamlets.

In their ships huddled captive girls in thrall for the long northern haul across kraken-swirled waters to womanless Iceland.

Amid terrible shouts, the warriors leapt into the surf and swarmed up the stony outcroppings to the monasteries.

The monks were hard men but poor warriors; half-mad from the rain and half-blind from copying in the dim light of tallow, they were no match for the Norsemen. They perceived the intruders to be a riot of evil set loose in the world to be tamed by prayer or perhaps appeased by offerings of boiled fish and chives.

The Vikings swatted away their frugal bowls and split the godly men from skull to pelvis with their battle axes.

Brother Mark watched as the marauders scaled the monastery walls, broke through the gates, and infiltrated the cloister. Nothing had changed in over a thousand years: it was still the same uneven match between good and evil.

The earth had circled the sun for a human eternity, describing its orbit through the ebony void; empires had risen and fallen; forty generations had been begotten and forgotten, and here was Brother Mark on the spume-soaked skellig, hearing the awful din of voices and clashing metal, the tramping of boots and promise of mayhem.

*G**et a load of fuckin' Scarface here.*
A fifteen-year-old whippet stood in front of Brother Mark, leering, tossing a crowbar from hand to hand.

Brother Mark gazed back at him, stone-faced, seeing a pig-eyed Norseman clad in sheepskin and wool. Brother Mark was holding an illuminated manuscript, a treasure dating from the tenth century. It was a marvel of intricacy and Celtic convolution, a splendid heir to *The Book of Kells*.

Amos strode onto the parapet and snatched the manuscript from Brother Mark. He inspected it, turning the exquisitely illustrated lambskin pages with admiration.

"This is some nice shit," he said. "Should be in the museum."

Brother Mark nodded.

"Then what do you have it for, Jack?" said Amos. "Huh?"

No response.

"Well, there's a new curator in town, buddy. This guy."

He thrust the manuscript towards a coarse youth with blunt fingers.

"Here," he said. "Rip it up."

The youth gripped the book and ripped it down the middle. He ripped it again, then again. He crumpled the pieces and threw them in the air, laughing.

Amos leaned towards Brother Mark, as if to tell him a secret.

"Not that it even matters, of course," he said, gesturing towards the sky, "but I'll have you know, Mr. Monk, that I thought that was a lovely piece of work. I am no barbarian."

Amos regarded the scattered pieces.

"The lack of symmetry is staggering. That book took lifetimes to make and only seconds to destroy. Quite a gradient, is it not?"

Brother Mark did not respond.

"Ah," said Amos, smiling, "the vow of silence." He turned to the whippet.

"You ever kill a monk?"

"No," said the boy.

"You ever smash a brain a thousand times more intelligent than yours? *You, who claim lineage from a flea,* have you ever killed a man with more virtue in his little finger than you have in your entire insignificant bloodline?"

The whippet was twitching. His fingers were white and pink where he gripped the crowbar.

"No," he said.

"Well, today's your lucky day, son."

Amos turned to Mark.

"Any last words, my friend?"

"Membrum meum suge," said Mark calmly.

"Say what, Jehoshaphat?"

"Paedicabo ego vos et irrumabo."

"Your prayers are wasted on me, monk boy."

Amos slapped the whippet on the back of the head. "Hop to it now! Whattaya think, we got all day?"

As clumps of bloody hair showered down around him, spotting the scraps of manuscript with red and black, Amos smiled at his work to see. He had orchestrated an act of perfect symbiosis: the boy was orgasmic in his resentful fury and the monk reached apotheosis as a martyr, purified for the Resurrection.

Amos missed, however, the greater irony. He never realized—except perhaps subconsciously, for as he abandoned the burning cloister, a jangly melody from 1969 insinuated itself in his head—that he had just ordered the death of someone whose end had been the subject of his own stoned ponderings: the fabled questing beast of the hippie mindscape: the vanished mandolin player of the Gigantic Waxworks Indelible.

Amos drove the herd of destruction across the canyon to the last remaining outposts of the elite. He found himself mixed in with a crush of migrants bent on revenge against those who paid them next to nada to groom their lawns and tidy up their obscenely opulent homes.

"Matemos a los ricos!"

Amos smiled, gracious, a shining Aryan in a muddle of jumbled pigment.

20

At her mansion, Mrs. Sexton was pouring what was to be her last glass of champagne. Although she—and everyone else present—was to die in an hour, she did not see the need to be a glutton.

"I have lived with restraint," she said. "I will die with restraint."

The first of many bullets whizzed past her fine patrician skull.

"Ah," she said. "So they have arrived."

Indeed, they had arrived—the barbarians, that is—at that most clichéd of locations: the gate. The walls were high—twelve feet—and fully capable keeping out the rabble—a role originally intended to be more symbolic than literal.

The mob, a mixed horde of Mongols, Saxons, Celts, Aztecs, and Zulus, were clamoring with swords, spears, and flame-spitting firearms, and set to tearing down the massive wrought-iron *portón* that stood imposingly across the drive.

Inside the gate, four-foot walls flanked the entryway, creating a narrow gravel sluice that channeled the way before it widened out onto the broader grounds.

As the mass heaved and strained at the gate, machine gun fire perforated the guard booth (abandoned) and an insolent salvo of several hundred rounds whistled uphill across the dry grass to strike the mansion itself, shattering windows and gouging out rough chunks of stucco.

I nside the mansion, the reaction to the fusillade was mixed. Some dived for cover, some manned the battlements, some continued unabated in their eating, drinking, or screwing. Some indeed picked up the pace.

Mrs. Sexton glided to the library with her champagne. Dying might be painful, but death, as far as we know, is not.

As she sat back in her chair, a slapping puncture of glass tinkled high up behind her, twinned a split-second later by another sudden *tink* in the big window opposite.

The first sprinkled inward, the second outward. Two sudden tinkles, two small drizzles of glass. With amused calm, Mrs. Sexton traced the flight path from one hole to the other.

"That would be Bede's silver sparrow," she said drily. "Fitting bookends for a life."

21

Upstairs, Lorenzo, his root raw from the mad rutting of Rapture, paused midhump to note the splintered glass showering down upon him, his oiled buttocks, and the woman glued to his underparts.

"Hey, what are you stopping for?"

She glared at him, sweating, ravenous—on her neck, a tattoo scorpion was pumping, pulsating.

"They're here," he said. "Shooting."

"Screw them," she said. "Screw *me*." She started pulling him down. *"You can't stop now."*

Lorenzo, though, was bored, finally—and for all time—with sex. His mind was drawn to the tumult outside.

A sudden volley of bullets teletyped a tattoo of the constellation Orion onto the wall. Plaster sifted down.

"Sorry, babe," he said, rolling off. "Party's over. It's time to fight."

She pushed him away irritably. "Go on then," she said. "Go on do your man thing and get yourself killed."

Another brisk volley nailed the Southern Cross up near the ceiling—a circular wall clock swung loose, scraped three times in a pendulum arc, and fell crashing.

Lorenzo, whitened as by the finest flour, calmly pulled on his baker's pants. His shirt was long gone, shredded like a windsock; his crucifix had also been bitten off somewhere. He walked out the door, unblemished, powder dusting his shoulders like snow.

The scorpion woman curled on her side and bit her knuckle. *O God, NOW what am I going to do?*

22

A few rooms down in the upper gallery, a fat Ugandan man was pressed against a narrow window, firing away with an assault rifle. He cursed profusely, his blubber and speech jolting with every shot.

His syllables jiggled out of him as if he were skateboarding over cobblestones. "Pi-ece of sh-it mo-ther-fu-ck-ers! Pie-ces of sh-it!"

On the bed was another gun, an AR-15 with a scope, and a pile of loaded magazines.

"Hey, guy," said Lorenzo. "You using this?"

"No! Use it!"

With the rifle butt, Lorenzo knocked out the next window slit and surveyed the grounds. No one had breached the walls yet, but the gate was swaying dangerously under pressure from the mob. Smoke and fire rose from behind the wall, suggesting burning cars and scorched grass.   Defensive gunfire popped from the rhododendrons below, and the legs of prone defenders were sticking out from among clumps of giant wild rye. His truck was still parked atop the driveway, skull keys in the ignition, pointing downhill.

Lorenzo locked in a mag—and maintaining tight muscular aim, funneled it off rapidly at the gate. When the fumes drifted off, he detected a dramatic shrinking of the enemy line. He was impressed. Bodies were down, blood flowing.

A shout from the fat man.

"They're on the wall!"

Lorenzo looked. Sure enough, heads were peeping over the wall, exploratory, tentative, identifying the bush-popping fire flashes. The Ugandan uncorked a volley at them, chipping dust and bursting off the top of one boy's skull. Lorenzo snapped in another mag and picked off heads like tin ducks in a shooting gallery.

23

Downstairs on the patio, the party had not hitched in its swinging stride; its members remained unruffled by both the approaching gunfire and a rising wind, the harbinger of the comet. Were it not for the dead trombone player sprawled across the flagstones like a dropped suit of clothes, his limbs awry and blood zigzagging from his chest like a crumpled tie, there would have been nothing at all amiss with the scene. Just another garden party at day's end, charmed by golden sunbeams and glittering crystal.

I n the library, a stray bullet had also snipped the wick of one of the viola players, and so the quintet became a quartet. "Opus 135, third into the fourth," said the leader quietly. *"Lento assai, cantante e tranquillo."*

Across the nave, Marisa closed the book in her lap, a finger still marking the spot. Page fourteen of *The Tibetan Book of the Dead*. Those lights in the *bardos*—blue? yellow? green? pearl? She looked around vaguely for a bookmark— and then smiled. She'd just have to wing it—a bit too late to cram for the afterlife. Focus on just one thing—*one thing only*. And she believed she knew what that was.

24

L orenzo, the baker's son, teeth clenched and gun blazing, was brilliantly forging a new epithet: defender of the tribe. Elation flooded his veins. The invaders, numberless, surged repeatedly against the gate, and the impeccable Lorenzo, from his second story sniper nest, rapidly papped them down.

Bullets sparked joy off the pinging black iron, scattering flak and thinning the heaving horde. Lorenzo's sizzling bullets erupted from the backs of the attackers—exploding lava and bones—leaving steaming-caldera exit wounds.

With every trigger-pull and with every mad marauder crumpling at the end of his smoke-bleared vision, Lorenzo felt himself becoming more and more male. Two weeks of solid copulation had not been enough: it took the blood-rush of the fight, the atavistic thrill of the kill, and the bitter metallic bite of adrenaline on the tongue—to make him fully Lorenzo.

His senses were so sharpened, so acute, and so efficient in their consumption and appreciation of stimuli that the whole world slowed, slowed, and slowed again—slowed like some unplugged, worn-out carousel, enabling him to examine at leisure every corner of his vision.

The approaching bullets were laughably large—as fat as spiraling footballs—and he easily ducked them with time to spare. If he'd had a smoke, he would have lit it up. He was godlike, untouchable; he had nothing to fear.

His Olympian vision expanding, Lorenzo regarded the brass casings of the discharged bullets with aesthetic enchantment. In slow motion, they traced graceful arcs above in the air, springboard divers tumbling end over end, their patterns echoing and overlapping before clittering down. A golden fountain, rising and falling.

At the far end of the drive, the rioters too rose and fell. In wave after wave, they were slamming against the gate, surging to some height, and then, shot, falling back on their comrades, arms out, spent, flotsam on the tide.

25

The sky became strangely bright; the wind turned savage: the end was at hand. Palms trees, their fronds ripping and lashing, crashed to the earth, their root-balls popping out like onions. The comet, not far away now, was blinding, a second sun, hard upon the pale of the moon's orbit; by the time the earth had revolved a few further degrees it would be, anthropocentrically speaking, all over.

Lorenzo, sensing the onrush of doom, the slick hiss of the falling blade, decided to go over the top in the fine Flanders tradition. After all, what was there to lose? Twenty minutes of life? Ten? Five? Bullets, the comet, a knife—what difference did it make?

The quick reel of his life spun him a winner—*nonna, risata, motociclo*—and in the last several days he'd done it all: he'd cranked like a miller and gotten his plums pounded into pudding; he'd gorged on Persian sherbet heaped in goblets of Waterford crystal—and been cross-eyed drunk on thousand-dollar wine; he'd had his white baker's uniform ripped buttonless by bacchanal maenads raving fifty shades of grape. He was, in short, ready to kick it—ready to give up the spark. Bring it on, Marcus!

It was Valkyrie time—strike up the music. He reloaded his rifle as well as that of the Fat Man—now dead, a bullet having whapped him cleanly in the forehead—and ventured stealthily outside. In the wind, the truck was shuddering like a horse. *Go near, join thyself to this chariot.* He jerked open the driver's door and peered down at the gate.

It groaned and bent one last time under the weight of the inexhaustible underclass and collapsed onto the gravel drive. Wild with victory, the mob stampeded over the fallen barrier and into the funnel leading to the grounds.

Lorenzo's flash: Cork the bottle, block the pass. *Charge. Thermopylae, baby.* He shot a quick triangle of holes into the windshield, kicked out a yield-sign, and gunned the truck down the hill. Through the ragged hole streamed a Toblerone bar of smoke, stinging his eyes—and over his ringing ears, the wind roared tympani and trumpets. *The glory of God thundereth, full of majesty.*

Before the throng could scatter, Lorenzo was hard upon them, steering with an uplifted knee—and through the flying-tiger grin in the glass, he unleashed his last trick: a withering spitfire barrage from his two firearms.

The truck was topping fifty by the time the first stunned raider punted high off the fender.

He ran them down like rats, serpents, heaps of squid, smashing them on the grill, lurching over heads, tails, hips, hyoids; crunching toppled torsos—wrapping legs, lungs, and screaming lips around the churning axles—blasting, shooting, striking, dragging, mauling.

S word in hand, Amos Flint pushed through a clot of shouting man-buns and took four, five, six shots to his chest before looking up to see the distinctive logo of the Ford Motor Company blur into red-tinged focus and strike his face. The sword bounced high and away.

A fat black wheel burst Amos like a grape, rupturing his organs and shoving them up through his mouth where they erupted in a jelly-welter of tongue and blood.

Like a wingless kamikaze, the Japanese sword flashed spiraling over the scrum and scored its final fatal hit through the eye and skull of a pink-haired rioter with a spiky anime doo. Her mouth remained open in amazement. *Oh.*

The truck forged on, carving its swath of karmic mayhem. A heap of torment—a vast multitude by wounds disfigured. Lorenzo, having lumped and bumped over some two dozen buccaneers, and rapído-pocked as many more, was finally felled himself when three gunmen stood still long enough to pump ninety rounds into the cab, only one of which was necessary to kill the baker's son.

Although pierced by twenty-nine bullets, it was the third bullet—the one that had entered his wide open, uvula-wagging mouth, grazed his tongue, and blown a hole through his medulla oblongata—that actually killed him.

A single bead of blood gathered at the bottom of his right earlobe—swelled, trembled, and then dropped.

In the fat neck of the narrows-gate, the truck had bucked up to a tilted stop on a terminal moraine of dead and dying bandits, groaning and squirming and oozing—the bullet-pocked truck sitting high like the sesame-seed top slice of a giant Italian hero—and Lorenzo, tipped back in his seat, white as a sugar-powdered Easter cake streaked with carmine, sat open-mouthed, beatified, gazing out through the miraculous wind-hole to heaven.

26

Qelvin Lee, still disoriented and unnerved by his façade-cracks of mercy, had been in no hurry to reach the top of the hill, and approached the gate after the bodies had piled three deep under the weight of Lorenzo and the Fat Man's massacre.

From across the street, at the bottom of a bluff of smoldering grass and scrubby trees, he'd seen the bread truck bull its Pamplona path through the cramped crushing crowd—and Lorenzo's sacrifice: *Well hast Thou fought.*

The myrmidons now streamed over and around the truck like ants over a loose plug in a bottle of molasses. These too were being shot down— but still they came. And were shot down. But still they came.

Bringing up the rear, Qelvin had neither fired his pistol nor so much as hurled a curse. Having put much of this madness in motion, he was feeling—if not compunction—strangely off-keel and weary. *Zozobra.*

Qelvin noted the violent winds and the unnatural cast of the sky: he was impressed that the end was really coming. He had never really doubted the doomsday reports, but it is difficult to take the Apocalypse seriously when the skies are blue and the swallows are flitting back to San Juan Capistrano. Nothing means anything except personal history.

But now it was here: the skies of California were going forever, blotted out by darkness, soot, smoke, and wind. The eye of the second sun was growing huge and fierce, glaring at the depredations of these last days.

F eeling emptied-out, drained of rage, Qelvin decided to pass on the final assault and witness the End from the top of the fire-streaked hill. As he climbed the graceful slope, he seemed to see two, even three, horizons moving in churning, burning cross-currents—a crimson gyre, a riptide parallax.

Some final revelation was at hand.

He hadn't climbed much farther before he stumbled upon the sunken den of a homeless man who, terrified, sprang upon him and stabbed him in a cornered rat frenzy. By the time the man had finished and jumped away, charcoal-faced and hissing with fear, Qelvin had a dozen holes in him and was close to dying. He was mute, surprised, and strangely serene. His vision began widening, rising.

How odd, he was thinking, bleeding, drifting away like a balloon above, *to be stabbed dead on this hill, by a wild man, a brother, his hair violent and wind.*

27

As the last breath left Qelvin's body, the gale kicked up another notch, sweeping debris of all classes into the air. Mrs. Sexton, having emerged from the library, and gripping a column for support, looked across the estate to see an airborne midden-in-the-making whipped along on the breeze:

Lobster shells, lawn chairs, hats, jackets, brassieres; steel drums, flowerpots, bicycle wheels; music stands, mannequins, dwarf stunted oaks—winged pages of *The Watchtower,* an alligator purse; hostas, hydrangeas, long streams of smoke; and, sandblasting all the air—dust, chafing dust—anything not nailed to earth.

She was pleased that the gale was also keeping the enemy at bay: staggering drunkenly against the wind and offering easy targets to the riflemen under the bushes. Perhaps no Cato after all. She turned back to the party, and to her library, preferring to die among beautiful things.

Passing her ranks of praetorian books, and re-throning herself inside, Mrs. Sexton gracefully drew up her legs beneath her. She took in the long nave of her chapel to the word and exhaled quietly. In the wind, the structure was groaning, a ship heaving through a storm, but the vessel was well-joined and would make the passage. The quartet was still aswim in the Beethoven—seated and swaying with closed eyes. Mrs. Sexton too closed her eyes.

And then the strings struck a crucial chord: she instantly saw how it would all end: the vision was brilliantly clear—a film, a dream, a memory engraved—it had already happened. The snake was seizing its tail again. She began to reach for her pen but then stopped with a laugh. In about five minutes, she would see this—exactly:

*T*he mansion exploding like a star, a supernova, and then, a split-second later, the library too exploding—a massive bunker-bomb, an Alexandrian brick-burst of dynamite tightly-scrolled, the 87,000 books shot like birds from a cannon—bindings blasted, pages flapping and fluttering—gusting like goose feathers;

And then, fireball and furnace roar—a blizzard of pages turning swiftly to fire—the whole roofless dome a chimney of heat—sun-bursting chairs, tables, ottomans, walls:

In a flash, she incinerates—a skeleton, a lightning strike—and yet, still she sees:

Pages spinning, flaming, gold and red—and wild flamencos whirling carousels, mushroom gills, into drunk and shrunken anthracite: fire-paper shrinking, withering and wasting—a million tiny mummified faces;

She sees black butterfly wings imprinted with hieroglyphs: fractures of words, phrases, calligryphs— alpha and omega, hamza and alif—slashes, strokes, signs, serifs—

And then, in a rush, all sucked away in smoke and soot, obliterated and transliterated—the Word made flesh made Word again—so much ash chasing down the wind.

And the glory of God thundereth, and great is His name—over chaos and storm, deserts and cities, over the featureless face of the deep; and as the whirlwind wanes and fires fade, hear now the voice of the Lord prevailing over the wide and murmuring waters.

Mrs. Sexton remained with her eyes closed for another minute. That is how it would be. Almost exactly like that. She knew it. Something had come through there—fertile, unbidden: she'd learned to trust such visions. The quartet played on with the Beethoven. *Muss es sein? Es muss sein!*

She opened her eyes—shadows of trees were bending and moaning across the windows. That last part, though—the voice, the waters— she would not have written that: a different narrative, a different geography. East of the Palatine, Attica, Ephesus, the blasted cedars. Could be nothing, could be something—she'd have to remain open to that. Marcus would.

She looked up at the clock. In three minutes, she would know.

28

Outside on the patio, in the shelter of an archway, Marisa stood hugging her flapping gown. The wind was blowing hard from down the valley, carrying on itself the last rumble of riot and destruction from the city below. All was wind and dust.

She closed her eyes to the fire and the storm and turned towards the music, one hand at her ear and the other under the very gentle swelling of her belly—a near-invisible increase, an offering—her crescent pietà.

D ean and the band played on, their music stands long since blown away. The wind sucked the notes from their horns and sent them howling. Breathing was difficult and listening futile.

The stand-up bass, exposing too much surface to the gale, was ripped from the bassist's hands and sent booming and thrumming across the stones and then veered wildly around the corner of the mansion.

The trumpet player leaned upwind from Marisa, his hair whipping and the notes leaping from his horn twisted and writhing, snapping in and out of her hearing like the cries of screaming birds.

29

D ean was at the center of the storm, reaching his musical peak. The blasts rushed over him, snapping at his jacket and tearing at his scalp, but he was ecstatic.

He pressed ahead like a mountaineer reaching the summit in snowy heights. Smit with love of sacred song, he caught the notes flying past him and gave them order, creating sanctuary in the wild evening.

T he rioters gained the upper driveway, having finally killed all the defenders in the bushes. But they could go no farther: the ferocious winds stopped them where they stood, crouching, grimacing, ninety feet from the patio. They shot blindly into the tempest. The bullets traced wild paths, striking columns, kicking up spurts of hard earth—giddy birds, ineffectual.

The earth shook wildly; the comet had struck. The wind blistered and the sky burned for five miles up. A tsunami of fire roared across the ravaged city, consuming the cud of its twice-burned ash and twisted steel.

The rioters stumbled and cursed, their hair aflame and eyes seared with the promise of the abattoir they would never gain. Wailing, gnashing of teeth—bootless cries to deaf heaven. In the inferno, they crawled and wept for their lost slaughter—and in a final grasping, shot at each other as they burned.

Dean was, in the closing moments of history, a happy man. His entire life-hoard of joy and beauty and pain focused itself into a single blinding point—an atom as bright as a star.

Unlike the quaking millions huddled in doomed basements, staving off the inevitable by a minute, an hour, or a half-day of pointless time, Dean picked himself off the stones and placed the horn to his scalded lips—the last horn to the last lips anywhere on the planet—and played a fiery song to the lost and the doomed.

The one or two players who still had instruments staggered after him, their jackets smoking as the sirocco burned their hair and singed their eyebrows.

And, just moments later, as the fire-ball raced up the canyon—and the grass, trees, and mansion exploded into flame—*déjà vu*—Dean rounded up their errantry one last time and pitched them all headlong into immortality.

He was catapulted beyond death, beyond the abyss into some remote and lightless place where there existed nothing but rhythm: the rhythm of time without end, of the tides of eternity rising and falling outside the cognizance of man.

The violence of the world's last days—the rape, the murder, the flailing against the dying of the light—they were all distant to him now, receded beyond the pale of Dean's awareness.

Even as his body burned, incinerated in a swift second by the towering column of fire, Dean was beyond all sense or feeling. He was beyond the world, deep in some dark and hidden end of the universe where all of eternity turned on an unseen pivot—the center of nowhere, utopia, a grand place, sacred, and full of wonder.

THE END

DREW'S WAR

A Vietnam War Tale

Da Nang, 1967

things out there

you wouldn't believe—

let me tell you

Drew Doles

PFC ANDREW DOLAN BAGUELLES
1st Battalion/7thCavalry/U.S. Army
Libr. Cong. No. 066/715/65DD
Nat. Archives/Oral Hist./efc

Tape rolling?

All right, let's hit it.

SO THERE I WAS, HANGING FIVE OFF A LONG BOARD, CHINA BEACH, Da Nang, soaking up some R&R after thirty days of hell in the bush. The surf was rolling in sweet and green, and my Gordon & Smith was snug under my feet.

The last few days of the tour had gotten hairy, real hairy. It was out in the Ia Drang, Pleiku province, where the 1st Battalion, 7th Cavalry got itself into a brutal firefight in the jungles a couple miles from the Cambodian border.

We'd gone out there with orders to find, engage, and destroy the enemy—that was our mission—and man, we had found them. Four battalions of them, three NVA and one Viet Cong, all heavily armed with the latest Russian hardware.

The whole shitstorm had gone down at LZ X-Ray, a sunburned patch of dry grass and termite hills amid the vines and tangle at the foot of the Chu Pong massif, Charlie's HQ.

For three days and three nights me and the boys of Bravo company, 1st Battalion, traded blood and death with the NVA, who came streaming down the mountain in wave after wave, eager to kill and willing to die. Lots of our guys got chopped up, good guys, all of them, but Charlie got chopped up a whole lot worse, ten to one by the body count.

We busted up Charlie good at X-Ray: we mowed him down with M-60 machine guns; we whacked him with grenades and mortars and blew him out of trees with rockets; we shot clip after clip from our M-16s on full automatic; we called in can after can of napalm and fried us up some crispy Viet Cong *au gratin.*

Even though we smoked him good, even though we whacked him hard, he kept coming. He kept surging at us through the tall grass, with his pith helmets and AK-47s and potato-masher hand grenades with wooden handles. Death was no deterrent to Charlie. You couldn't kill him fast enough.

That's when we called in the B-52s. We radioed for a bomber strike out of Guam and on the third day, a whole squadron came rumbling up the valley like distant thunder, a stack of crucifixes five miles high.

Armageddon time. From 5,000 feet to 35,000, there was nothing but big birds dropping payload after payload of 500-pound bombs all over Charlie and up and down the Chu Pong massif. The whole valley shook and heaved and tossed rocks and trees in the air. At the same time, the artillery was still whistling in with shell after shell of HE and Willy Pete—

BAM! BAM! KA-BAM!

——We were bouncing around our foxholes like pieces of popcorn. Back at Fort Benning, we'd been told that textbook too-close on an artillery strike was four hundred yards; at X-Ray, we pulled it in to forty yards because that's how close you had to bring it if you wanted to stay alive in the Ia Drang.

But that's not the story I meant to tell you. This next one is. But first, a little bit more of this lubricate the muse.

Much better.

Definite improvement.

To the gods.

ALL RIGHT. SO THERE I WAS, OUT ON MY LONG BOARD, CHINA BEACH, thinking about everything that had gone down out in the shadow of the Chu Pong. It was hard to believe I was even alive. One day I'm in LZ Hell and the next day I'm in the green room, having tea with the Pope. Hard to get your mind around shit like that.

The surf was sweet: ten-foot glassy tubes, more barrels than a brewery. Good stuff and everything. The sun felt good: bright and hot and sparkling like diamonds off the tops of the waves. You could look out to sea and almost believe you weren't out here in a war.

That's always a big mistake in the Nam—forgetting you're in a war—and I got jacked back into the facts real quick by some strafing machine gun fire that tore a line of white across the waves in front of me: a whole volley of bullets perforating the green.

A quick glance over my shoulder and I see a couple Viet Cong hunched down on the dunes, squinting down the sights of a 60 mm Maxim, spitting out three hundred rounds a minute. Time for some quick evasive action: I duck down and cut back along the curl—not an easy spin on a long board.

I'm crouching low, hissing along, and then unclip my .45 from its ankle holster and fire two shots over my shoulder. Each shot whacks a guy between the eyes and they both topple back on the dunes, dead.

The tube's coming at me so I plant the skeg again and cut down the drop and work it out fast along the curl, beginning to think I might be able to ease back into some good surfing, but that's my second mistake: there's no such thing as an easy ride in the Nam. No sooner have I whacked those guys than two more take over the gun—and then, after I had whack them, two more and then two more and then two more. I'm whacking them two by two, like Noah's Ark in the shooting gallery. *Pop! Pop!* Two more! *Pop! Pop!* Two more!

Charlie finally catches on that I'm not going down easy, so he fans out along the dunes and in a minute there's a whole company of VC letting rip with AK-47s and dropping mortars on my ass, making me slalom in and out of the bomb blasts like a demented snowboarder.

After some more E&E, I take the offensive again—in a big way. I told you before I'd been hanging five off my long board; I would have been hanging ten except I was weighed down with a fully rigged, battle-ready M-60 machine gun, complete with tripod and hundred-yard strip of armor-piercing bullets. Charlie doesn't have any armor, but that just means more fun for me. I reposition my feet, swing the gun into place, and let fly, watching Charlie's heads pop off like champagne corks on New Year's Eve.

Even though the body count is large, real large, Charlie keeps coming, hundreds of them, just like he had done in the Ia Drang.

Things take a turn for the worse: A line of machine gun fire comes boiling across the glass, grazes me in a bunch of places, and saws my board in half. I manage to stay up on the back end, but my blood's dripping in the water and the salt's stinging like a bitch.

It was right about then, right that minute, that Charlie began to piss me off. Not only had he put a cramp in my R&R; not only had he cut me up with a half-dozen bullets, making me bleed; but he had also shot up my favorite board, my sweet, customized Gordon & Smith, the one that had scooped me a silver at the World's, Steamer Lane, Santa Cruz, 1963. *My Gordon & Smith, do you understand!* F*ckin' Charlie!

Pissed now, I mow down another wave of VC, and then swing the M-60 back behind me the way Elvis used to swing his guitar. I reach into my camouflage trunks, pull out an M-79 grenade launcher preloaded and ready to fire, and get busy. *No more Mr. Nice Guy.* I let fly with the M-79 and grenades start exploding all over the beach like it's the Fourth of July.

It looks like things are going my way but that's my third mistake: thinking things are going my way. You can't afford to do that in the Nam.

Next thing I know, there's a big crunch by my feet and look down to see the jaws of a fifteen-foot tiger shark munching down on the remains of my championship board, his nasty-looking crooked teeth an inch from my foot.

A quick look around: nothing but sharks. The whole area, from the inside break, through the fizz, and out past the outside break, is packed tight with sharks, thousands of them, sniffing out my blood and slicing up the surface with their shiny dorsals. Shark City, ten years before Benchley. I hadn't heard the music over all the gunfire.

I turn the M-79 on the sharks, blowing up tigers and makos and hammerheads, raining down teeth and chum and chunks of flesh. I clear me a little perimeter but also churn up a vicious feeding frenzy from all the blood. There's jaws and teeth flashing and grinding.

A tough situation: sharks in the sea, VC on the beach—not much of a choice, but all told, I figure I stand a better chance against Charlie.

The best way to get off the water A-SAP immediately on-the-double pronto is to employ the old Central Highlands rocket launch trick—something I'd learned from the Green Berets out in An Khe. I pull out my fifty-foot coil of nylon rope, tie one end of it to the rocket, right above the fins, and loop the other end around my waist. I then load the rocket into the M-79, adjust it for weight and distance, and fire it up at a 51-degree angle due west and *BAM!* *WHOOSH!* I'm soaring through the air, ducking from the back blast, towed by the rocket up over sea and surf and sand and dunes. I cut myself loose seconds before the rocket explodes and tumble into a sandy somersault behind Charlie's position.

I jump up with the M-60 blazing, and gun down everything in sight, from Charlie to the sandpipers all the way down to the fiddler crabs. The body count was large.

When the firing was done, the beach was quiet, real quiet, and there was hardly a sound except for the wind, the ringing in my ears, and the heat clicking off the barrel of the gun.

Slowly, wearily, like Odysseus after the wars, I policed the battlefield, counting the dead and checking for wounded. There were no wounded; I had whacked them all. I left all the bodies where they lay and took a walk along the shore to look for some fragment of my board, toeing among the bits and pieces of shark that were sloshing in and out on the pink tide. I couldn't find any.

I squatted down on my haunches, Vietnam
style, and gazed out over the South China Sea.
A couple thoughts drifted through my head:

I am going to miss that board.
I am going to miss this war.

NOTES ON COMPOSITION

$$2^2 + 3^2 + 4^2$$

AT THE END OF THE WORLD: The earliest form of this tale—the core 70% or so—was written a good while back in The Bronx. It started with the first sentence, which has remained. The story was revisited later, on the island of Patmos, and again in 2012, for a reading by Andrew Neuman at the storied West Harlem jazz club, Sakevino (Mr. Kevin Fitzgerald Burke, proprietor); the occasion was the Mayan *fin-del-mundo* 12.12.12. Midnight came and went without incident. The story slumbered again for another nine years and was then further revised and substantially expanded in both 2021 and 2023 during the COVID-19 era. Though it could probably be expanded yet again, for now, Dean and the others will stay where they are, spinning and riffing in the whirling swirl of eternity.

DREW'S WAR: Composed on the sands of China Beach, Da Nang, Vietnam; also on the banks of the Ayeyarwady River, Bagan, Union of Myanmar, in the company of three intrepid balloonists and the nimble monkeys of Mount Popa. Came upon a midnight clear when reading *We Were Soldiers Once … and Young,* by Lt. Gen. Harold Moore, U.S. Army.

In memory of the great Drew Doles., U.S. Army, surfer, bandmate, blues-punk harmonica player, master storyteller, dear old friend, Jersey Shore, USA.

ABOUT THE AUTHOR

T ED CLEARY is a writer and artist from The Bronx, New York. He has had an interest in the Apocalypse since reading the Book of Revelation on the South Island of New Zealand, where, short of cash, he camped out on a carnivorously swarming black-fly beach miles downslope from snow-capped mountains. Years later, he laid his head in the stone hollow carved into the wall of the cave on Patmos where tradition says Saint John the Divine had his revelation. Three days of fierce, white-capping winds followed, making all travel among the Aegean islands impossible. Delayed on Patmos, he revisited and revised *At the End of the World* while brisk pink octopi, pinned to fishermen's clotheslines like gesticulating undergarments, dried and dangled in the Mediterranean winds.

OTHER TITLES

SONG OF THE CICADA

"This does for the short story 'Araby' what *Ulysses* did for *The Odyssey*." — F. O'Sullivan, *The Phoenix*

A novella set in teeming Flushing, Queens, in a summer of thunderstorms and sweltering heat, *Song of the Cicada* explores the inner and outer worlds of a teenager transformed by overwhelming attraction for a tantalizingly out-of-reach girl. Rich in texture and detail, and keen, subtle recognitions, this story accurately evokes a young heart coming alive to sensations and insights.

While its germinal DNA traces back to the grandmaster Joyce and his story "Araby," by the time the novella is done, it's traveled so widely across time and oceans and continents, putting down roots in foreign soils and picking up new odors and flavors— that it's become another species of flora altogether.

"Marvelous. A gem on every page. The Kama Sutra sequence is a gasping fictional moment." — Michael Seidel, author of *James Joyce: A Short Introduction*; Advisory Editor of James Joyce Studies; Prof. Emeritus of English and Comparative Literature, Columbia University

"The prose has a wildness and lushness reminiscent of the Joyce of *Ulysses,* or maybe Flann O'Brien or Rushdie ... Phantasmagoric."
— Matthew Wikander, Distinguished Prof. Emeritus of English, University of Toledo

"Very beautiful evocation of a life in a place with rough edges, one that wouldn't ordinarily lend itself to evocations of celestial unity. Highly polished, very well observed—the street scenes in particular."
— James H. Kunstler, author of *Young Man Blues*

Excerpt: Her image accompanied him even in places most hostile to romance. Wandering down Roosevelt Avenue on the long June afternoons, on breaks from the suffocating store, he would weave his way among the jostling crowds and see her face in the air before him as if from behind a veil of lace.

Down the sidewalks he moved, sidewalks burning with midday glare, and yet he glided unruffled, a shadow across the sea. With her face before him, shining like a chalice, nothing bothered him, nothing disturbed him from his dream. With perfect serenity, he sailed among and above the street life of Flushing: he sailed past the buses starting up with high-pitched whines, blowing their gusts of hot exhaust across his calves; he passed the sidewalk preachers proclaiming the good news of the Lord Jesus Christ through crackly megaphones.

He lingered by the Peruvian street musicians playing their sweet airy tunes on pan pipes and guitar; he skirted the squatting Chinese ladies selling batteries, *bok choy,* and small green turtles swimming round and round their plastic bowls. He crossed in front of a homeless man slumped in the recessed window of a bank. He gave smooth and easy berth to the gently swinging feet of a man sitting on a wall, seemingly entranced and writing in a notebook, his heels bumping to some internal pulsing rhythm. With the heat damp and close around his skin, he passed the pizzeria with its A/C grinding out even more heat onto the sidewalk, a heat dense with the smell of mozzarella and garlic; he stepped past the OTB parlor with its chain-smoking men in crooked glasses studying the racing forms and staring with brittle hope at the live feed from Belmont Racetrack; he glided around the small wide women hauling orange shopping bags and trailing two or three weeping and tottering children.

He smiled on his walks now—he smiled because there had been times when he'd bristled among the throngs of Main Street, times when he'd felt hemmed in and harassed, harried by the noise and the fumes and the squealing of bus brakes; by the heat and glare off the cars jamming up the intersections; by the drivers pounding their horns as the lights turned from red to green and then back to red again, nothing moving, everything gridlocked, the pedestrians surging around the cars like the sea heaving and swirling around the humpbacked rocks of the strangled shoreline.

TEENAGE WILDLIFE: DAVID BOWIE

Less a biography of the iconic rock star (1947-2016) than an exploration of a listener's early immersion in the music, this idiosyncratic essay teases out—and weaves back together—diverse strands of Bowie's songs and persona, the author's 1980's Bronx Irish-

Italian culture, and riffing associative meditations on art and immortality. There's energy here, and color and spark, but the center holds, just as Bowie's songs adhered to classic form even amidst their flash and strut of Ziggy Stardust.

Composed immediately following Bowie's death in Jan 2016, and touched up lightly later, "Teenage Wildlife" is both a homage to an audacious artist and a rediscovery of those islands of memory that exist, at times half-forgotten, in every listener's experience.

SNAPSHOTS OF BELARUS: MINSK

Chronicling a train journey from Moscow to Minsk, in a backdoor quest to get a friend's Russian visa renewed, this short travelogue pairs scrupulous observation with occasional Gogolian turns, in keeping with the spirit of the former Soviet bloc.

Excerpt: A little later, in the vastly empty park of the white memorial, an old woman entered, hobbling slightly, and sat down at a nearby bench. I nodded to her, but she did not appear to see me. She was bundled in a brown ochre coat with her stockings rolled up just past the knee. She appeared to be in her late sixties or seventies—which would have made her a little girl during the war—but appearances can deceive here in Belarus, and in Russia, where people—and just about everything else—weather quickly from the long cheerless winters.

She opened her bag and took out a box of cigarettes, its logo a pale blue disc encircling a black bull's eye. She lit a cigarette, turning away from the wind and hunching slightly to protect the flame. She carefully placed the spent match on the bench and then leaned back to relish her smoke.

And relish it she did, for hers was not a casual smoke: it was a serious and mindful smoke—a scrupulously intense, closed-eyed drafting deep into her lungs (and then retaining it there for several seconds) as if she were aspirating the very fumes of paradise.

When she inhaled, she cocked her head slightly towards the sun, a heliotropic plant, and puckered her lips to drag fiercely at the butt. Her cheeks crumpled from the strain, and the wrinkles of her mouth aligned tightly like the grooves and folds of a paper umbrella.

She sucked with such vigor that it seemed the cigarette were smoking her instead of she the cigarette, and then suddenly she flew up—head, body, boots and all—and disappeared into the butt of the smoke, sucked like a doll into a vacuum cleaner. The cigarette then flipped upward, end over end, a sparkling pinwheel, and finally landed with a surprised shock on the footpath, where it was scrutinized briefly by red-toed pigeons with abruptly swiveling heads.

To Dream, This Costs Nothing: Notes from the Underground, NYC

If we had any idea what we were doing—if we had perfect knowledge of all the ripple effects, of every last flap of the butterfly wings—we wouldn't do what we do. But alas, we don't—and so it goes. A tale from a New York summer, and of the mischief that idle hands can play. The devil's workshop indeed.

NOTE ON THE TYPE

T his text is set in Dragamond, a post-Renaissance serif typeface admired for its elegant line, subdued emphasis, and classic search for transparent form. It was first cut in Copenhagen, 1674, by Amundi Magnússon, the only surviving child of Guðbrandur Magnússon, a young blacksmith abducted from Iceland in a 1627 slave raid by Barbary pirates, who captured 250 Westman islanders and sold them into bondage in Algiers. The raids, entering Icelandic history as the *Tyrkjaránið,* were chronicled by the Rev. Ólafur Egilsson, an older cleric inthralled along with Magnússon.

In Algiers, sundered from his teenage wife (sold to an Ottoman seraglio), Magnússon labored nine years in a Moroccan foundry, grudgingly perfecting his metalworking skills, until a local plague and palace fire enabled his escape to Corsica, and then to France, Holland, and finally Denmark, where he settled in Copenhagen. Neither his wife nor Iceland would he ever see again.

Establishing himself as a punchcutter and printer, he remarried and had five children, four of whom died in nursery, and the final child, Amundi, short of sight but gifted of craft, mastered metals, matrices, and punchcutting under his father, absorbing Parisian typographical styles and fashioning at least twelve distinct moveable types, Roman, Nordic, and Gothic, including *dragamond* (named for a Slavic patron with draconic heraldry).

Attaining wide renown, Amundi had only just seen the birth of his daughter (who would grow to be a great beauty), when during a communiqué crisis in the Scanian War, the Danish admiralty pressed him into service as first printer of the Baltic fleet. On July 2, 1677, during the Battle of Køge Bay, amidst a maneuver and exchange with two Swedish warships, Magnússon, retrieving a spyglass for the post-captain, stepped out into the wind and smoke of the quarterdeck, adjusted his spectacles, and was instantly killed by an exploding shell.

For further titles, please see the author's Amazon page

tedcleary.studio@gmail.com

tedcleary.com

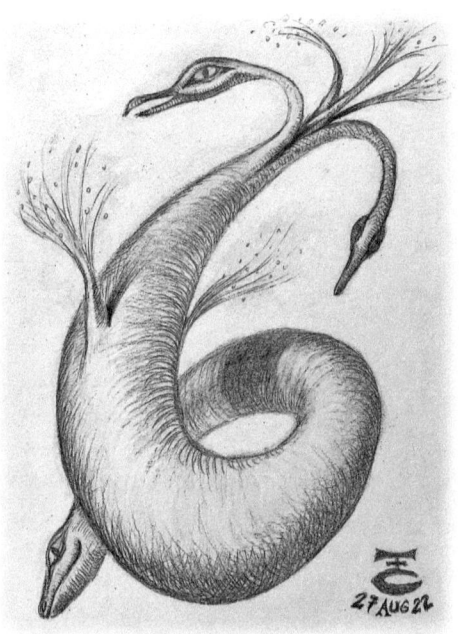

www.ingramcontent.com/pod-product-compliance
Lightning Source LLC
Chambersburg PA
CBHW051958170626
46808CB00007B/2676